FINDING FIRE

Logan S. Kline

CANDLEWICK PRESS

To Hunter,
Enjoy the
Adventure!

Logan S. Kline

This is for Kim, Braelen, and Alden.
While the world changed around us, you helped
me make something beautiful.

~

First edition 2022

Library of Congress Catalog Card Number 2021953119
ISBN 978-1-5362-1302-7

22 23 24 25 26 27 APS 10 9 8 7 6 5 4 3 2

Printed in Humen, Dongguan, China

This book was typeset in Arno.
The illustrations are a combination of graphite, ink, oil paint, and digital techniques.

Candlewick Press
99 Dover Street
Somerville, Massachusetts 02144

www.candlewick.com

Long before the secrets of fire
had been discovered, people had to find fire.
And if they lost it . . .
if it went out . . .
someone would need to search for more.